tiger tales
5 River Road, Suite 128, Wilton, CT 06897
Published in the United States 2020
Originally published in Great Britain 2020
by Little Tiger Press Ltd.
Text and illustrations copyright © 2020 Jane Chapman
Visit Jane Chapman at www.ChapmanandWarnes.com
ISBN-13: 978-1-68010-189-8
ISBN-10: 1-68010-189-7
Printed in China
LTP/1400/2939/0919

For more insight and activities,
visit us at www.tigertalesbooks.com

I Love You with all my Heart

by Jane Chapman

tiger tales

Little Bear was playing the drums.
"Look at me!" she shouted.

Ba ba boom! BASH! BANG!

"Wow!" laughed Mommy.
"What a bouncy beat!"

The drumming went
on and on . . .

faster and faster . . .

and louder and louder . . .

until—

CRASH!—

Mommy's favorite plant
was in pieces!

"Oh, no!" gasped Little Bear, staring at the mess.
"Mommy will be so upset!"

"I'm sorry, Mommy!"
Little Bear sniffed.
"Oh, sweetheart — it's okay,"
smiled Mommy kindly.
"But it was your favorite!"
sobbed her cub. "And now you'll
be sad . . . and angry . . .
and you won't love me anymore!"

Mommy pulled Little Bear close.
"I'll ALWAYS love you," she said.
"Put your paw on my heart, and
you'll feel my love beating on
and on forever."
So Little Bear did.

Ba ba boom.

Ba ba boom.

"It beats in your heart,
too," Mommy whispered.
"Can you feel it?"

"I can!
Just like a drum!"
giggled Little Bear.

"Remember,"
said Mommy with a kiss,
"my love will always
be with you wherever
you are."

Mommy was right. Her love was there
at school the very next day.

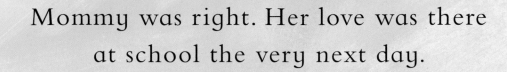

"I'm going to win!" giggled Little Bear,
racing her friends to the finish line.

But when Badger
overtook her with a

"Wheee!"

Little Bear's feet just
couldn't keep up.

Her breath began
to hurt in her chest
until—

Whump!

she flopped down on the grass.
"I want my mommy!" Little Bear sniffled.

But then Little Bear remembered what Mommy had told her. She put a paw on her chest and —

Ba ba boom
  Ba ba boom —

Mommy's love was right there in her heart!

She wiped away her tears and started to smile. "I'm proud of you for trying so hard," said her teacher. "Let's have a snack while we wait for Mommy."

Later, back in the yard,
Little Bear was excited to fly her new kite.
"Yippee!" she cheered, rushing
into the wind.

But a strong gust tugged the string
right out of her paw.

"Come back!" she cried as
the kite sailed away.

"My kite is gone!" whispered Little Bear sadly.
But then she placed a paw on her heart
to feel Mommy's love.
"I will find that kite," Little Bear decided,
and she marched across the grass after it.

Dangling from the tree
on the other side of the yard
was a tail!

"My kite!" laughed Little Bear.
She rushed to grab it . . .

. . . but slipped —

Splash!

— right into a puddle.

Little Bear shook
the mud from her fur.
"Puddles won't stop me!"
she declared and began to
climb the tree.

Up went Little
Bear, higher
and higher.

"I can do this!"
she mumbled,
her heart beating fast.
Then, holding on tight,
Little Bear reached out as
far as she could . . . .

"Got it!"
Little Bear couldn't wait to tell
Mommy, so she raced back across
the yard to find her.

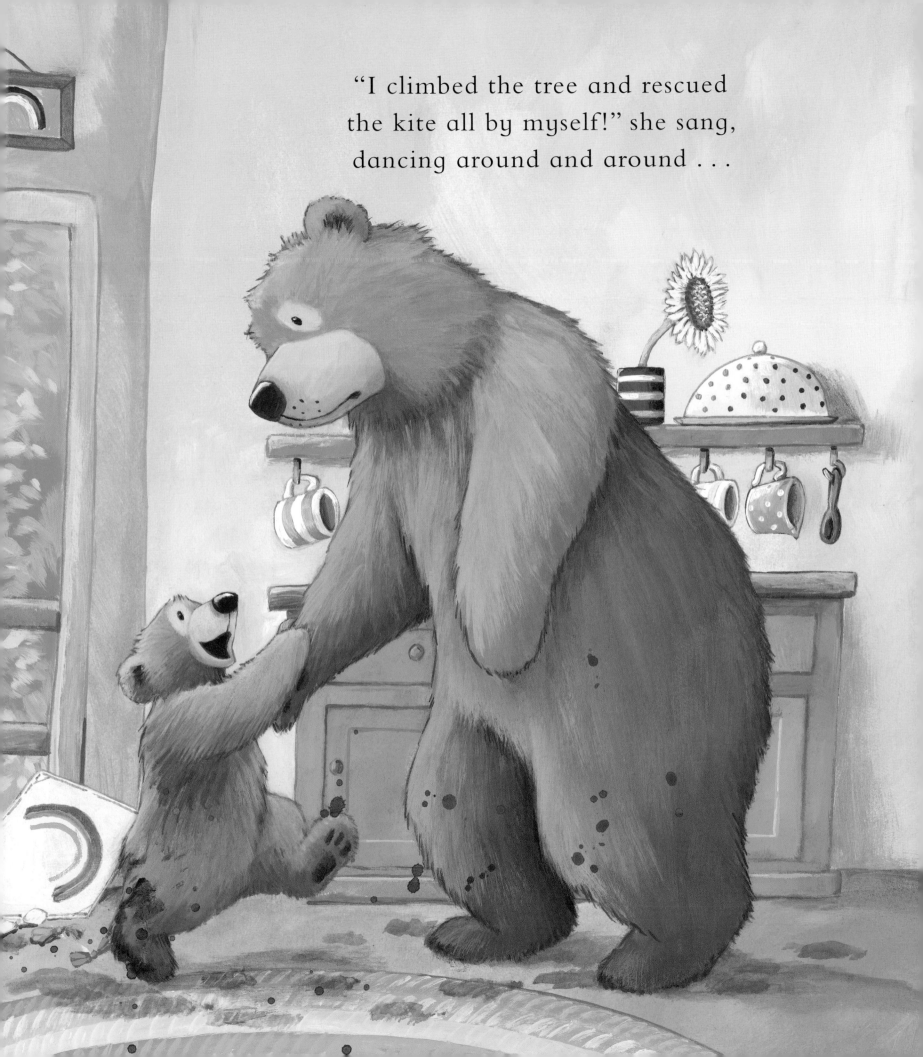

"I climbed the tree and rescued
the kite all by myself!" she sang,
dancing around and around . . .

. . . and leaving muddy pawprints
EVERYWHERE!
"Oh, Little Bear! What a mess!"
cried Mommy.
"Outside with all that
mud, please!"

Little Bear put her head in her paws.
"Nothing is going right!" she sobbed. "I broke the flower,
and lost the race, and now I've made
you dirty . . . and upset!"

Mommy scooped Little Bear into a cuddle.

"Sweetheart, there were good things, too,
like playing the drums and saving your kite!"
she whispered. "And even when I'm upset,
I still love you with all my heart. Can you
hear it beating now?"
And Little Bear could!

Ba ba boom.
Ba ba boom.

"I made you a surprise,"
beamed Mommy.
"Are you ready?"
She reached into the oven, but . . . .

"Oh, no!" she sighed sadly.
"I burned the cake!"
Little Bear took Mommy's paw
and led her outside.

"Even when things go wrong,
I still love you," laughed Little Bear.
"Put your paw on my heart, and you'll see."
"Wow!" said Mommy with a smile.
"It's FULL of love! Just like mine!"